Toto and his bone

Om KIDZ

An imprint of Om Books International

Om KIDZ | Om **Books International**

Reprinted in 2021

Corporate & Editorial Office
A-12, Sector 64, Noida 201 301
Uttar Pradesh, India
Phone: +91 120 477 4100
Email: editorial@ombooks.com
Website: www.ombooksinternational.com

Sales Office
107, Ansari Road, Darya Ganj
New Delhi 110 002, India
Phone: +91 11 4000 9000
Email: sales@ombooks.com

© Om Books International 2015

ISBN: 978-93-84119-45-4

Printed in India

10 9 8 7 6

Toto and his bone

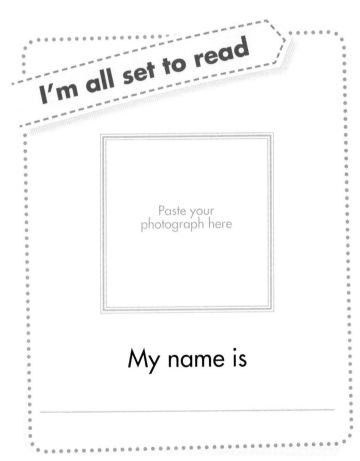

Paste your
photograph here

My name is

_____

Toto was looking for
his bone.

He looked under the pillow.

He looked under the bed.

The dust made him sneeze.

He looked under the carpet.

But there was no bone.

"Let's go to the garden, Toto," said Candy. Toto and Candy went to the garden.

Toto looked for his bone under the tree.

A little bug bit him on the nose.

Toto still couldn't find his bone.

He dug up the leaves.
But his bone wasn't there.

"What are you
looking for, Toto?"
asked Candy.

Toto wagged his tail hard.

"Come on inside. You are so dirty! I need to give you a bath," said Candy.

Toto had a bath and went to his basket to sleep.

And what do you think he
saw in his basket?
Yes, his bone!

Toto happily went to sleep
with his bone beside him.

Know your words

Bone – Something that a puppy loves to chew.

Pillow – A soft cloth bag stuffed with cotton or feathers, for us to lay our head on.

Dust – Dirt in the air that makes us cough.

Sneeze – A feeling when something tickles our nose.

Carpet – A piece of cloth we lay on the floor.

Garden – A lovely green place full of grass and flowers.

Bug – A tiny little insect.

Leaves – Green things that grow on trees.

Basket – Something that holds things.

Wagged – Shook from side to side.